For  Jo

First published 2009 by Walker Books Ltd
87 Vauxhall Walk, London SE11 5HJ

This edition published 2024

2 4 6 8 10 9 7 5 3 1

© 2009-2024 Lucy Cousins

The right of Lucy Cousins to be identified as author of this work has been
asserted in accordance with the Copyright, Designs and Patents Act 1988

This book has been typeset in Gill Sans MT Schoolbook.
Handlettering by Lucy Cousins.

Printed in China.

British Library Cataloguing in Publication Data:
a catalogue record for this book is available from the British Library

ISBN 978-1-4063-7736-1

www.walker.co.uk

Little Red Riding Hood

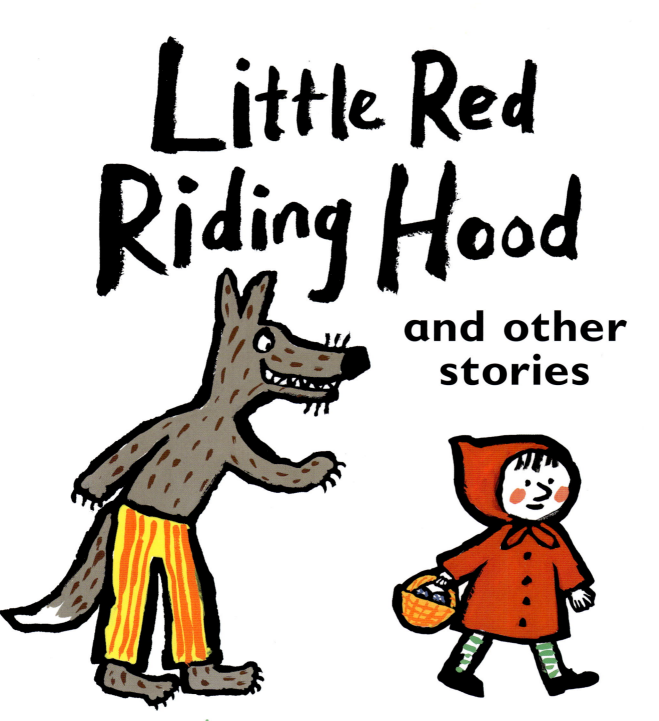

and other stories

Lucy Cousins

WALKER BOOKS
AND SUBSIDIARIES
LONDON • BOSTON • SYDNEY • AUCKLAND

Little Red Riding

Once upon a time there was

a girl called Little Red Riding Hood.

Her mother asked her to take a

basket of food through the wood

to her grandmother, who was ill.

Hood

Little Red Riding Hood had not gone
far when she met a wolf.
"Where are you going, Little Red
Riding Hood?" the wolf asked.
"I am taking a basket of food to
my grandmother, because she is ill,"
answered Little Red Riding Hood.
"Is that so?" said the wolf with a
nasty grin and away he ran.

The wolf ran straight to Grandmother's
house and knocked at the door.

"Who's there?" called Grandmother.

"It's me, Little Red Riding Hood," said
the wolf in a sweet little voice. "I've
brought you a basket of food."

"Come in then," said Grandmother.

gulp

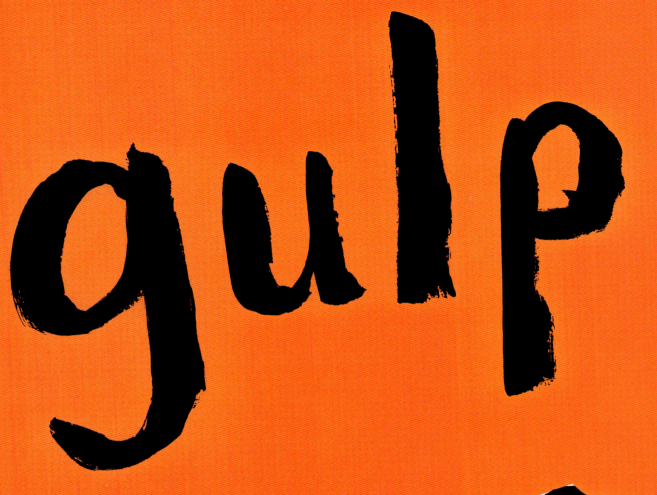

The wolf went in, leapt on to Grandmother's bed and swallowed her whole.

After a while Little Red Riding Hood arrived at Grandmother's house. She walked straight in and over to the bed.

"Grandmother, what big eyes you have," she said.

"All the better to see you with, my dear," replied the wolf.

"Grandmother, what big ears you have."

"All the better to hear you with, my dear."

"Grandmother, what big teeth you have."

"All the better to eat you with, my dear!"

And with that the wolf leapt out of bed
and gobbled up Little Red Riding Hood.

A hunter was passing and heard
the noise. He came in and
saw the wicked wolf.

chop

He chopped the wolf open
and out stepped Grandmother
and Little Red Riding Hood.
"HOORAY!" they cried.
Then they ate up the food
in the basket and lived
happily ever after.

The

Three Little Pigs

Once upon a time there was a
mother pig with three little pigs. They
were so poor that the mother pig sent
the little pigs away to seek their fortune.

The first little pig
met a man with a
bundle of straw.
"Please, Man," he said,
"give me that straw to
build a house."
Which the man did and
the little pig built his house.

please, Man

Then along came a wolf who knocked at the door.

"Little Pig, Little Pig, let me come in."

The little pig answered, "No, no, by the hair

of my chinny chin chin!"

So the wolf said, "Then I'll huff and I'll puff

and I'll blow your house in!"

And he huffed and
he puffed and he
blew the house in
and ate up the
first little pig.

The second little pig met a man
with a bundle of sticks.

please, Man

"Please, Man," he said, "give me those sticks to build a house." Which the man did and the little pig built his house.

Then along came the wolf and knocked at the door.

"Little Pig, Little Pig, let me come in."

The little pig answered,

"No, no, by the hair of my chinny chin chin!"

So the wolf said,

"Then I'll huff and I'll puff

and I'll blow your house in!"

And he huffed and
he puffed and he blew
the house in and ate up
the second little pig.

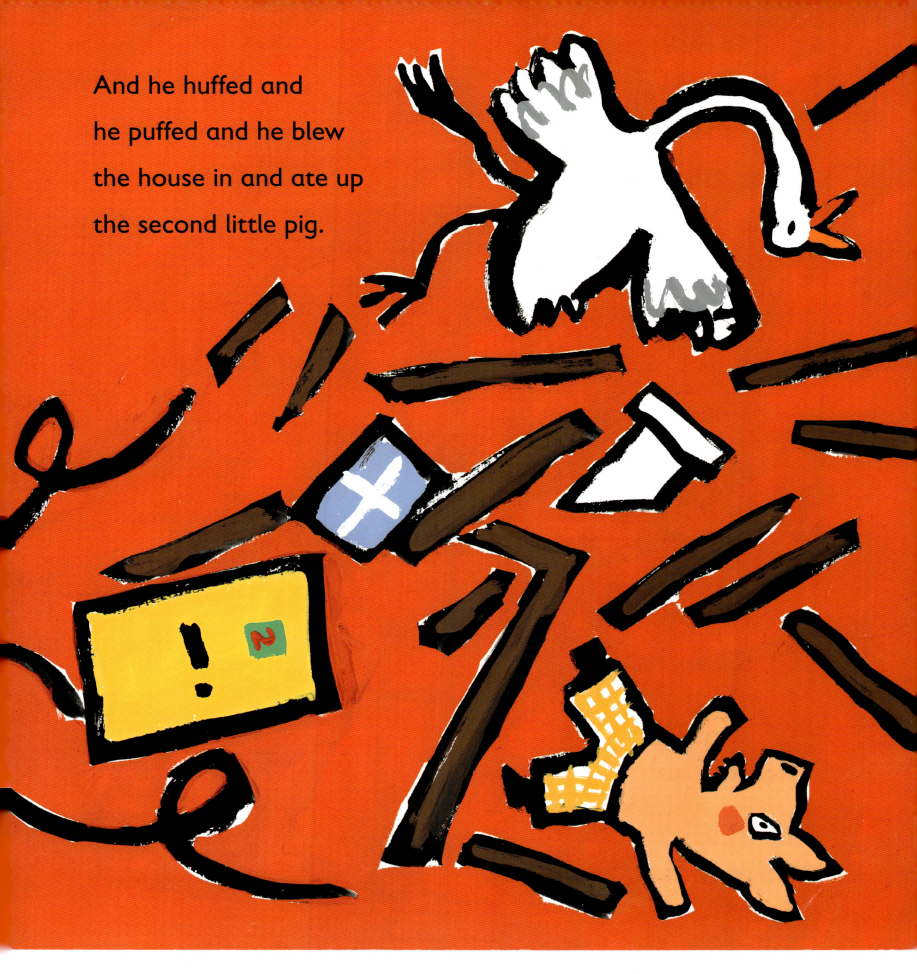

huff puff

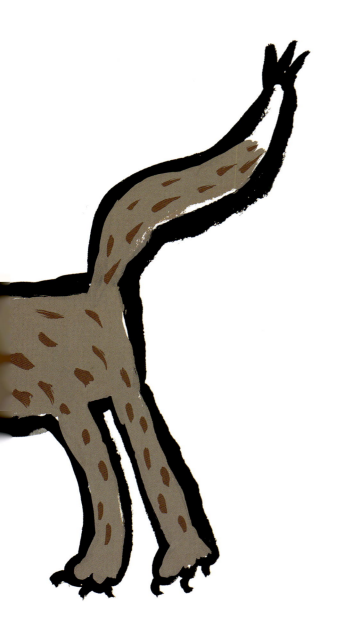

Then along came the wolf
and knocked at the door.
"Little Pig, Little Pig,
let me come in."
The little pig answered,
"No, no, by the hair of
my chinny chin chin!"
So the wolf said,
"Then I'll huff and I'll puff
and I'll blow your house in!"
And he huffed and he puffed,
but he could not blow the house in.

The wolf was very angry.

"Little Pig," he said, "I'm going to climb down your chimney and eat you up!"

So the little pig made a blazing fire and put a huge pot of water on to boil.

grrrr

As the wolf was coming down the chimney, the little pig took the lid off the pot and the wolf fell in. The little pig put the lid back on and boiled up the wolf and ate him for supper.

The little pig lived happily ever after.

bye-bye, Wolf

The Enormous Turnip

Once upon a time an old man wanted to grow turnips, so he scattered some seeds on his garden and said, "Grow, seeds, grow. Grow into big juicy turnips."

The next morning the old man went out to the
garden and found that one enormous turnip had
grown. But when he tried to pull it up, he pulled
and he pulled but it wouldn't come out.

"Dog, Dog, help us pull up the turnip," called the girl.

They pulled and they pulled.

"Cat, Cat, help us pull up the turnip," called the dog.

They pulled and they pulled.

"Mouse, Mouse, help us pull up the turnip," called the cat.

They pulled and they pulled and they pulled ...

they pulled and they pulled

and at last out came the turnip!

hooray

They took the turnip
home and chopped it
and cooked it and had

an enormous feast
and they are probably
still eating it now!